Logansport Cass County Public Library P9-ASK-413

LOGANSPORT LIBRARY

1501 9100 242 528 5

J F AUE

Auerbach, Annie.

Hero copter

Hero COPTER

By Annie Auerbach   Illustrated by Isidre Mones and Steve Mitchell

LITTLE SIMON
An imprint of Simon & Schuster Children's Publishing Division
New York   London   Toronto   Sydney   Singapore
1230 Avenue of the Americas, New York, New York 10020
Copyright © 2004 by Mattel, Inc. MATCHBOX and all associated logos are trademarks owned by
and used under license from Mattel, Inc. All rights reserved.
LITTLE SIMON and colophon are registered trademarks of Simon & Schuster.
All rights reserved, including the right of reproduction in whole or in part in any form.
Manufactured in the United States of America
First Edition
2 4 6 8 10 9 7 5 3

Logansport-Cass County Public Library

Steve Kiley loved to fly. In his twenty years of being a pilot he had probably spent more hours in the air than on the ground. Up in a helicopter he felt like a bird and loved looking down on the world below. Being a helicopter pilot with a search-and-rescue team was a perfect job for him. For there was only one thing Steve loved more than flying—rescuing people in trouble.

602263

"Good morning, everyone," Steve called out as the Friday shift began.

"Good morning, Birdman," Aimee teased. Steve liked to be in the air so much hat he had been given the nickname "Birdman."

Aimee was the rescue swimmer, and Nate and Glenn made up the winch rew. Since the search-and-rescue team worked together for twenty-four hours at time, they knew how to tease one another!

Logansport Cass County Public Library

Before Steve even finished his morning cup of coffee a distress call came in. A plane had crash-landed into the trees of the Shandy National Forest. The pilot had jumped to safety but his leg was broken. He had radioed for help. Emergency assistance was needed—fast!

"Time to fly!" said Steve.
Without wasting a second, Steve, Nate, and Glenn were off.

Steve hurried into the cockpit of the helicopter while the winch crew got into position. When they reached the rescue site, Glenn would be hoisted down on a long, steel cable called a winch to reach the pilot of the downed plane. It would be up to Nate to control the lowering and raising of the winch from the hovering helicopter. One thing was certain: teamwork was essential!

Logansport Cass County Public Library

Steve flew the helicopter toward the forest. The rotor blades on top sliced through the air, giving the helicopter lift. Steve loved how a helicopter could fly up, down, backward, and forward. It was the perfect rescue vehicle and he used its capabilities to their fullest potential.

Soon Glenn spotted something silver stuck in between the towering redwood trees.

"I think that might be the plane, Birdman," he said to Steve over his microphone. Inside each safety helmet was a microphone, so the crew could talk to each other.

"Confirm that," replied Steve and he began to maneuver the chopper downward toward the enormous trees.

As the helicopter descended, Steve made sure to keep a safe distance from the branches of the trees. By keeping the rotor blades of the chopper tilted at a medium angle, Steve was able to hover just above the tops of the trees.

Meanwhile Nate lowered Glenn down with a stretcher to rescue the injured airplane pilot. Once he was securely on the ground, Glenn detached the stretcher from the winch and radioed for the helicopter to move away to reduce the noise level. Since a helicopter can fly straight up—no runway needed—Steve maneuvered the chopper away and waited to hear from Glenn.

Glenn was a trained emergency technician, so he quickly examined the pilot and determined that he had a broken leg *and* a fractured shoulder. He helped the pilot onto the stretcher and then radioed through his microphone for the helicopter to return.

But his radio wasn't working!

Thinking quickly, Glenn went to an open area and set off a flare to signal the helicopter to return.

"That's my cue," Steve said and immediately flew back to the rescue site.

Nate hoisted Glenn and the injured pilot as Steve maintained a stable hover with the helicopter. Once everyone was safely inside the helicopter, Steve headed for the nearest hospital.

"Nice work," Steve told the crew. "It would have taken a ground crew a lot longer to get through that forest."

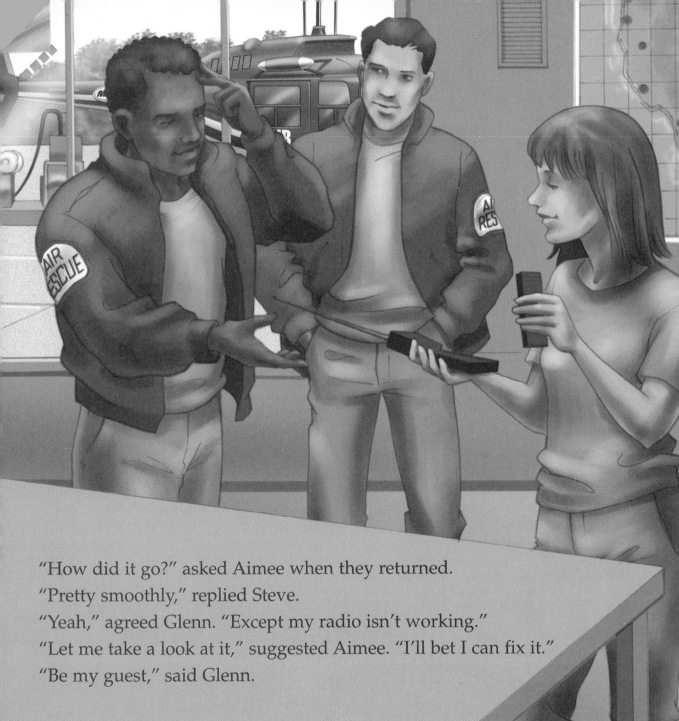

"How did it go?" asked Aimee when they returned.

"Pretty smoothly," replied Steve.

"Yeah," agreed Glenn. "Except my radio isn't working."

"Let me take a look at it," suggested Aimee. "I'll bet I can fix it."

"Be my guest," said Glenn.

Later that day Aimee told Glenn and Steve that she was able to fix the radio. Then Steve checked the weather report. "Sounds like a storm's coming," he reported to the others.

"Looks like it too," said Nate, peering up at the sky.

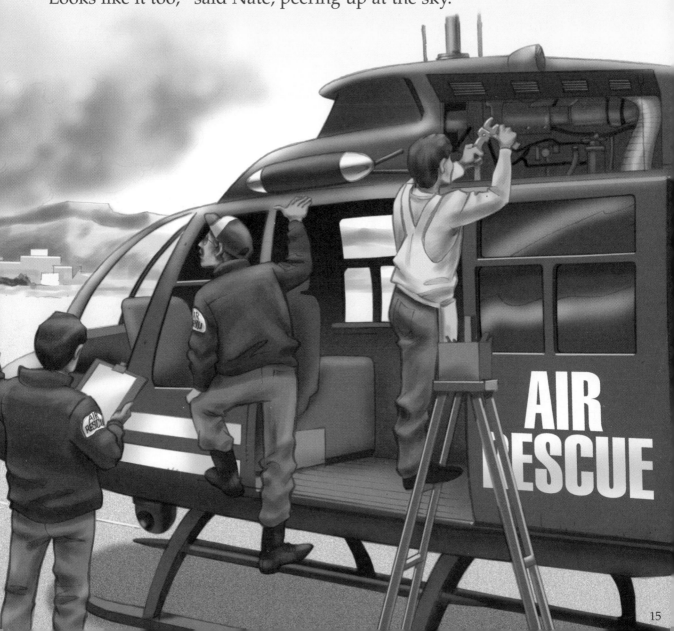

Meanwhile out in the ocean a father and his two sons were finishing up a good day of fishing. The wind began to blow the dark clouds and the waves began to rise.

The father hoped that they could make it back to shore before the brunt of the storm hit. He tried to start up the boat, but the engine wasn't working.

CRACK!

Lightning crackled across the sky and rain started to fall. Waves began to break, with the water coming up fast and furious. A huge swell overtook the boat and it began to fill with water!

The father knew there was only one option left—call for help.

"Mayday! Mayday!" he radioed, as more water flooded the boat. He radioed their current position.

Would someone be able to find the family in time?

The search-and-rescue team heard the Mayday call over the radio. Steve, Nate, and Aimee ran to the helicopter in the rain. It would be difficult to spot a boat in these conditions, but nothing was going to prevent the rescue crew from trying!

Once in the general area of the disabled boat, Nate used a forward-looking infrared (FLIR) camera to try and locate the stranded fishermen. This special equipment relied on identifying the heat of a person's body.

"I've spotted them!" Nate announced.

Steve carefully maneuvered the helicopter directly into the wind in order to get the best hover capability.

Down below, the family was relieved to see the helicopter rescue crew. The chopper arrived on the scene quicker than any boat could have!

When the helicopter was in the best position, Aimee was lowered down in a hoist to the deck of the boat. Nate then winched down a rescue basket and Aimee set about getting one of the sons in the basket. She gave a thumbs-up to Nate to begin winching him up. Soon the other son was hoisted up too.

"Two down, one to go," Aimee said to herself.

Aimee motioned for the father to get in the basket when suddenly a huge wave crashed over the ship. Aimee grabbed onto the rail but the father wasn't so lucky. Man overboard!

SPLASH!

Aimee dove into the water. At first she couldn't see the father but then she spotted his life jacket. Aimee swam to him and pulled him back onto the boat.

Before long the father and Aimee were hoisted up
to the helicopter, safe and secure.

By the end of their shift the next morning the crew had rescued six people total. Everyone was eager to get some rest. Well, almost everyone.

"What are you doing on your day off?" Aimee asked Steve.

"Going flying, of course!" Steve said with a laugh. He couldn't wait to get up in the air again.

Aimee laughed. "Say hello to the birds for me!"